T0365796

# Elle
## the
# Sea Captain

4Pixiedot

AuthorHouse™ UK Ltd.
1663 Liberty Drive
Bloomington, IN 47403 USA
www.authorhouse.co.uk
Phone: 0800.197.4150

© 2014 4Pixiedot. All rights reserved.

No part of this book may be reproduced, stored in a retrieval system,
or transmitted by any means without the written permission of the author.

Published by AuthorHouse 01/22/2014

ISBN: 978-1-4918-8807-0 (sc)
ISBN: 978-1-4918-8994-7 (e)

Any people depicted in stock imagery provided by Thinkstock are models,
and such images are being used for illustrative purposes only.
Certain stock imagery © Thinkstock.

This book is printed on acid-free paper.

Because of the dynamic nature of the Internet, any web addresses or links contained in this book may have changed
since publication and may no longer be valid. The views expressed in this work are solely those of the author and do not
necessarily reflect the views of the publisher, and the publisher hereby disclaims any responsibility for them.

authorHOUSE®

Pixiedot, my friend the mutant pixel, is an extraordinary traveller. His ability to slip through the layers of time make exploring with him an amazing experience. Today I am visiting this 16th Century fort. Pixiedot cannot resist old places, he sees an opening that is not visible to the human eye and with lightning speed he goes through. Pixiedot can recount details of past lives and events the likes of which you will not find in history books.

Pixiedot where are you and what do you see?

I see a very good six year old girl who lives in a fort next to a busy harbour town, Elle is her name. She is the foster child of the noble Earl of Desmond. Elle has no memory of where she came from or when she came to live with this happy family. Her first memories are of a missed heart beat and a yearning for adventure.

Elles everyday is the sand, the sea, the wind and the salty spray.

The handsome Earl, sporting a big mustache and his Spanish wife with her dark brown eyes, raven hair and wearing a gown of emerald silk, meander along the quay amidst the hustle and bustle.  His sailors unload heavy casks of fine wine and all sorts of goods from his ships into huge stores.  The fort is overflowing with sweet fancies and healthy joyous people, with music, laughter, song, and merriment galore.  Elle and her three brothers dance a wild jig to the harmonious sounds around them.

Memories come back to Elle and she is drawn to the Madonna in the walled garden. Seeing the vague face of her real mother in the statue a warm feeling spreads into her heart. A voice from within communes with the vision, words unspoken fill Elle with a sense of safety and calm. In these quiet surroundings she can see a way forward. A new strength energises her to forge ahead into the future on a voyage of discovery. Elle runs away from the garden happily.

A time of unrest spreads across the land.  Sentrys are placed ouside the town by the new governor. The family feel strange passing a sentry as they walk to the chapel for mass.  The Earl does not approve of the  new governor because some of his relations have been jailed without trial.

He says.  "Local people should not have to put up with the hardship caused by these unjust rules, it hinders their daily lives.  Our peaceful town and safe harbour are ruined!"

The priest spoke from his pulpit disclaiming the unjust rules brought on their heads by the new governor.  People gather outside in tight groups to share their fears and trepidations about such cruel governance.  Amid this crisis the Earls children are guided to their normal activities and go to the cloister for lessons.

Elle gives the task her full attention, well almost, her mind is elsewhere. Out at sea is where Elles mind is, thinking, the anchor, the wind, the tide, the sails.

Elle is growing up and she spends all her time on her boat called "The Clipper". There is trouble in the town, some families have left to save their lives. Elle and her crew enjoy the freedom which sailing brings to them. The actions of sailing, letting out the mainsail, changing the jig, manning the rudder and scrubbing the decks keep Elle and her crew fresh, active and healthy. This could be a saviour to them in the future. The crew know every cove, every rock and outcrop along the coastline.

15

Peter is the youngest sentry and unlike the other sentrys he is shy and polite.

Elle is very relieved when she sees him on guard.

Before long Elle and Peter become friends, they often talk for hours when the road is quiet and Peter is free.

Sometimes Elle will find any excuse to go into the town and at times Peter is seen in places where Elle is sure to be.

18

One day Rosalyn, Elles best friend, is visiting when a messenger arrives bearing an invitation to a banquet in the governors palace. The Earl thinks he should not attend saying, "I fear it may be a trap."

Elle agrees. "But." she says, "We must be careful not to offend thus giving the governor an excuse to be angered."

It is decided that Elle should attend the banquet on behalf of the family. "I will be safe." she assures them.

A beautiful silk dress is sewn. The bodice of the dress is superbly embroidered. On the night of the banquet there is great excitement in the fort. A coach is made ready, Elle will not be intimidated by the governor or his army, she will make a spectacular entrance.

As Elle passes Peter the sentry on the palace steps he whispers to her. "Meet me on the veranda after midnight."

Peter warns Elle of a plan the governor is forming with the army. It is a plan to destroy the Desmond family, leaving the way free for the governor to seize their stores and wine cellars.

"You and the Desmond family are in great danger." says Peter. "An army will raid the fort on the night of the full moon." he tells her.

"The governor has promised a prize to the soldier who captures the Earl"

28

The Earl heeds Peters warning knowing the governor is a wicked man. Spurred by fear and with great sadness a decision is made by the family to flee. They must work as a team to load the ships with their household goods. From every corner new and old sea chests are gathered.

In this foray an old chest belonged to Elle is discovered, it is the one which she arrived to the fort with many years ago.

Much will be left behind as it is nearly the full moon. Time is not to be wasted on selecting personal items, the children will bring only what they are wearing and can carry.

From the old sea chest Elle pulls a lovely warm cloak that smells of fresh sea air and as she does so from underneath it the glint of a strange looking ring catches her eye. Memories come flooding back to her and a fiery courage shivers her spine.

32

The family work hastily, even so much is to be left behind. "At first sight of the moon we must push off," says the Earl. "There is to be no delay." Sweating, heaving and shouting the sailors get ready. By the light of the full moon the small fleet is at sail.

When the army arrives at the the fort the ships are well out of reach. The soldiers swear at the ships and at each other, angry for having been denied their prize. "We will punish the one who betrayed us." they hiss.

The governor cares nothing for the Desmond family but is furious over losing the ships. Peter is charged with treason and will be punished severely, he is very frightened. An old sergeant pleads for Peter saying to the judge. "He is young and foolish my lord." and "It is the girls fault my lord, she tricked him." The court has mercy on Peter, his life is spared, instead he is sentenced to guard the fort day and night for the rest of his days.

Elle secretly returns to the fort through a secret passage, anxious and fearfull, hoping to meet Peter. She hears a shout.

"Who goes there!"

Terror run through her heart, she stumbles, looks up and sees that it is Peter.  Peter shouts down at her "I am ordered to shoot anyone on sight, how did you appear here?"

"Peter you can come away from here now with me,"  crys Elle.

"No." he shouts.  "I am a soldier, this is my life.  I must do my duty. I will not abandon my post."

Elle sails away, her heart full of anger, frustration, disappointment and shame.

Peter is punished for being kind and true. The Desmonds are forced to leave their beloved home.

Her strength fails her and she has to surrender to the waves. Elle lets the waves carry her to a shadowy place where she drowns in deep despair.

Then, suddenly, a crisp and happy voice comes from out of nowhere proclaiming.

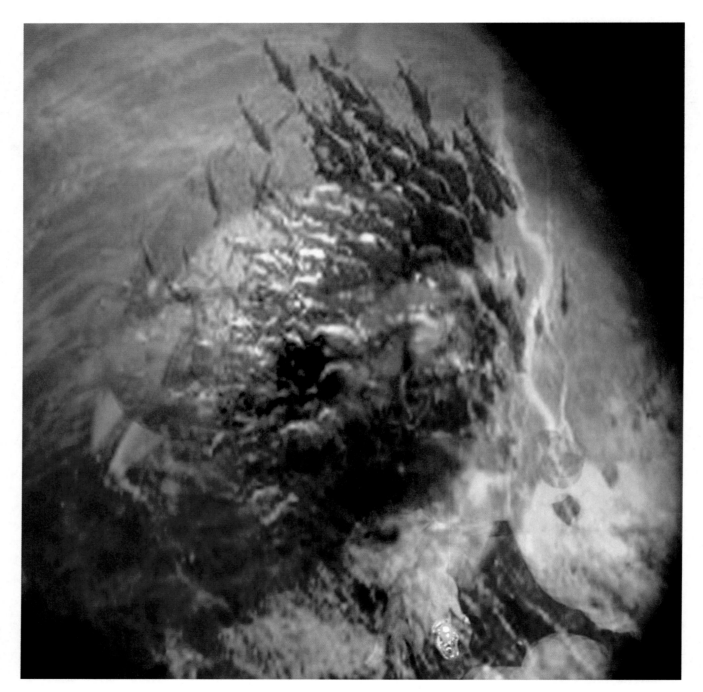

40

"Who so wears the queens ring has dominion over me and look how fair she be! "
A dolphin circles Elles lifeless body twice.
"As your king." says the dolphin, "To defend your gentle heart, I command you to put on this mask of pearly sheen so none can see your pain."
"Now, my queen." he continues, "Armed with your mask, cloak and ring of dominion o'er the sea, who will challange thee? "

43

# The End

Printed in the United States
By Bookmasters